This is book 1 in
a new series called

"THE ADVENTURES
OF DUMPSTER DOG."

Colas Gutman

Dumpster Dog!

Illustrated by Marc Boutavant

Translated from French
by Claudia Bedrick & Allison M. Charette

ENCHANTED LION BOOKS

NEW YORK

*Ben, who dug
Dumpster Dog
out of the garbage.*

Dumpster Dog Falls to Earth (with a Bump)

Dumpster Dog was born in a dumpy, old garbage can. There are many rumors about him: He might have been abandoned by his parents, he smells like sardines, and he can't tell his right from his left. All of them are true, but they're not even the half of it. Dumpster Dog is also covered with fleas and never goes anywhere without his fan club of flies. But beneath the mangy coat of this unfortunate creature, there lives a sweet and affectionate being who sees himself as something of a Labrador.

Sadly, his appearance—that of an old shredded carpet—drives even the most courageous children away.

Dumpster Dog shares his garbage can with his friend Flat Cat, a hard-luck cat who was flattened under the wheels of a truck at three months old. Flat Cat always wants to play the same games with Dumpster Dog—over and over and over again.

"Want to play *Cat and Mouse*?"

"No, I'm a dog."

"What about *Cat's Cradle*?"

"I'd prefer a nice bed."

Poor Dumpster Dog. He never understands anything. But one day, the discovery of an old shoelace in his garbage can pushes him to ask his friend a funny question:

"Hey, Flat Cat? Do you know why dogs have leashes?"

"Because they have owners, Dumpster Dog!"

"What are 'owners'?"

"You don't know what an owner is?!"

"No, I don't."

Suddenly, tears are streaming down Dumpster Dog's snout. He senses that an owner is something important, something every dog knows about except for him. To buck himself up, he gulps down an old banana peel and some expired yogurt.

"Please don't worry," Flat Cat reassures him. "I'll explain it all to you."

A can of liverwurst and three boxes of ravioli later, Dumpster Dog is dreaming of an owner who will love him and give him treats.

"Hey, Flat Cat? Do you think I'll ever find an owner in a garbage can?"

"No, Dumpster Dog. To find one, you'll have to roam the whole wide world."

Dumpster Dog promises Flat Cat that he'll come back soon, with a bicycle pump to re-inflate him.

Then, he sets out from his garbage can,
filthy as a pig and dumb as a donkey.

After mistaking a jump rope for a leash
and following two pigeons that he guesses
might be owners, Dumpster Dog sees
someone who seems just right.

Hopeful as ever, he thinks, *I'll offer him a few fleas to win his trust.*

Dumpster Dog nozzles the owner's leg, but he doesn't seem to appreciate it at all.

"Get lost, you old doormat!" snaps the owner.

"There are far, far too many flea-bitten tramps in this city," sniffs the well-groomed poodle next to him. "It's ridiculous."

"Oh, I quite agree," remarks a besweatered basset hound. "They're multiplying like rats! They should all be put down."

Suddenly, the owner stops and peers down at Dumpster Dog with a strange look.

"Are you out on the street all alone, shredhead? And are you really just a dog under that disgusting coat?" The owner roars with laughter.

I think he likes me! Dumpster Dog wants to howl with joy, but he can't make even the tiniest sound. He's so overcome by emotion that he feels like he has a package of peanuts stuck in his throat.

"Okay, you mangy dog, follow me," the

owner commands. "I'm going to take care of you!"

It's the best day ever of Dumpster Dog's dumpy life.

Treats! And toys! For me! he muses. *Which room is my owner going to give me? Will there be a TV where I can watch animal-rescue shows? And children to give me doggy treats?"*

Dumpster Dog is as excited as the fleas jumping around in his fur. But all that comes from having an owner is that he's planted outside a rundown gray little house, with a sign hanging around his neck that reads: "Beware: Smelly Dog."

That evening, the brave pooch devours the bowl of leftovers from the day before the day before yesterday that his owner has left for him. After, he flops down on the gravel like a sack of potatoes and falls asleep.

Later, as he's waking up—oh, joy!—his owner is there, asking him, "Did you sleep well, old carpet?"

"Very well, thank you," says Dumpster Dog.

"Good. Then we're going to celebrate! Come on—time to haul off somewhere special for lunch," snickers the owner.

Dumpster Dog chases after the owner's car. The well-groomed poodle and the besweatered basset hound are riding comfortably in the back seat, but Dumpster Dog

Dog is elated all the same. *What a fine owner to have me exercising so I'll stay in shape!*

Half an hour later, tired and thirsty, Dumpster Dog arrives at:

Dumpster Dog Falls Low

"What are you bringing me this week?" asks the butcher.

"Two little weenies and a mop," answers the owner.

"I don't want your mop. It smells like sardines."

"When do we get to eat?" Dumpster Dog asks.

"When pigs fly," says the owner.

"All of them?" asks Dumpster Dog. "I only know one . . ."

"Tell your mop to shut up! I'll take the poodle and basset hound for my cocktail franks."

"Deal," says the owner.

"No takebacks," says the cook.

"It's not fair," Dumpster Dog sniffles. "No one ever picks me." And he thinks, *I'm just a poor stray dog, a black sheep without a shepherd, an owl without a tree, a can without a can opener.*

The owner groans. "What's to be done with you? Okay, I suppose you can stick around as a guard dog. You're so ugly you would scare anyone away.

After a while, Dumpster Dog starts to feel a bit more cheerful and snaps up a fly. He likes his new job. Everyone veers away at the sight of him, even blind people, who are put off by his sardine smell. Only a few curious sorts dare to approach him.

"Are you a werewolf?" asks a woman.

"Or a sheepskin with legs?" inquires a man.

"I'm going carpet shopping," says an-other. "Might I take a small sample of fur?"

Dumpster Dog is beginning to miss the

tranquility of his garbage can, when he sees a girl approaching. *A child! I love children!* Like a magnet to a fridge, he is drawn straight to her.

I wish I knew the secret of making puppy-dog eyes, he sniffles to himself.

"Hello, doggy!" says the girl. "What are you doing here?"

"I'm guarding my owner's house," says Dumpster Dog.

"You're not scared of bandits?"

"Uhhh . . . What's that?"

"You're such a good doggy! Do you like beef treats?"

"Oh yes!"

Poor little girl, thinks Dumpster Dog. *Her sneakers don't even have shoelaces. But what's that in her hand? Treats?!*

"Here you go, nice doggy!"

Dumpster Dog gulps down the treats and instantly falls fast asleep, like he's been bitten by a tsetse fly.

While Dumpster Dog heaves and snores like some huge hairy beast, the girl lets the three bandits know that the coast is clear. Emerging from the bushes, they head for the owner's house.

One television, two computers, and five necklaces later, the scoundrels are wiping their feet on Dumpster Dog, mistaking him for a doormat. Naturally, the poor pooch wakes up.

"Oh look! My owner is bound and gagged in the backyard! He must be playing *Cops and Robbers* with me. I'll be a good police dog and set him free!"

"Slobbering idiot!" his owner shouts once he's untied. "Drooly fool! Sardine stinker!"

"Who's this foul fellow that's bothering you?" Dumpster Dog asks. "You should get rid of him at once!"

"It's you, you dumb dog," says the owner. "What good are you if you let burglars in?!"

Dumpster Dog Falls into a Trap

The owner puts a new sign around Dumpster Dog's neck: "FREE: One Lazy, Useless, Dumb, Dumpy Dog." But no one wants him, so after a week of swallowing flies and scratching his fleas, Dumpster Dog decides to go find work as a doormat at a restaurant. *When I earn enough money, I'll be able to buy a bike pump for Flat Cat and shoelaces for that kind girl!* he thinks, remembering his promise to Flat Cat.

Dumpster Dog sets off again, puffed up with pride and ready. Unfortunately, some kids mistake him for a soccer ball. He takes refuge in a restaurant, but is kicked out. Nobody wants him, not even as a part-time doormat. *I'm a shoelace without a sneaker*, he laments, *a pot without a handle, spaghetti without sauce, a dumpy dog in the dumps for life.*

But sometimes in the life of a dumpy dog, there are miracles, and Dumpster Dog spins around for joy when he sees a sign that reads:

Dumpster Dog has finally found a place that smells like soup and will accept him just as he is. A girl is there to greet him. *That's odd,* he thinks. *She looks exactly like the other girl. And look! She doesn't have shoelaces either.*

"Haven't we met somewhere before?" he asks her.

"I doubt it. I don't talk to mops or doormats!"

Dumpster Dog could have sworn he was right, but he knows his brain is like a boiled peanut, so he doesn't argue.

This is such a strange place, he thinks.

Peering inside, he sees a fish tank with two toads playing *Leapfrog* and a cage with some swans playing *Duck Duck Goose.*

Oh goody, Dumpster Dog thinks. *I'll slip inside and make some new friends.* But no sooner has he pushed open the door to one of the cages and set a paw inside, then a cat starts howling, "Watch it! You're stepping on my tail!"

"What?! Is that you, Flat Cat? What in the world are you doing here?"

"Dumpster Dog? Is that you?"

Before the two friends can say anything more, the girl with red sneakers slams the door of the cage, fastening it tight.

"I'm sorry. I have no other choice," she whispers. "You must stay right where you are, or my owners will kill you!"

"Your owners?" says Dumpster Dog. "I thought children had parents!"

The girl leaves without a word.

"Flat Cat, I think we're going to like it here. I can feel it!"

"Dumpster Dog, you're as clueless as you are dumpy and smelly. And you're a super smelly, dumpy dog!"

Dumpster Dog Falls into the Wrong Hands

Flat Cat has good reason to be worried: Their cage has now been packed into the back of a truck with other cages.

"We're going to get turned into dog food," says a lame duck.

"Or turtle soup," says a turtle with no shell.

"That sounds delicious!" says Dumpster Dog. "Oh, Flat Cat, you see? Isn't this fun? We're moving!"

"I don't see what's so fun about getting kidnapped."

"What are you saying? Who would want to kidnap us?"

"We would!" grunt the three bandits, guffawing.

"As for you, mangy old dog, we have something special in mind for you. Your smell interests one of our clients. So, we're gonna wring you out like a wet mop and make dog juice."

"Perfume, actually," says another of the bandits. "We're gonna call it *Parisian Dog.*"

"Did you hear that, Flat Cat? I'm going to be famous!"

But there's no answer from Flat Cat, who's now squished between an alpaca with no wool and a zebra with no stripes.

The truck drives to the edge of a forest and
stops in front of:

"Here we are!" the girl shouts.

The cages with the lame duck, the donkey, the mute parrot, the one-armed penguin, the turtle with no shell, and the wingless pigeon are the first ones out. The girl unlocks the cages and ushers all the animals into the museum.

Dumpster Dog is excited. "Wowie, a museum that welcomes dogs! Come on, Flat Cat! Maybe they'll have treats and even the *Mona Lisa*!

But Flat Cat has flattened himself to the side, hoping not to be noticed.

The first bandit says, "We're gonna sort you into groups."

The second says, "Some will get stuffed and end up in the museum."

The third says, "The rest will be sorted however we want."

"I'm so flat they'll hang me in a frame or turn me into a placemat," says Flat Cat.

"They'll probably turn me into a duck whistle," says the lame duck.

"And me into a clay pigeon," says the wingless bird.

"'Stuffed.' Is that when you eat a lot of garbage?" asks Dumpster Dog.

Inside the museum, Dumpster Dog sees the well-groomed poodle and the besweatered basset hound.

"Hello, old friends!" he calls. "How's your kind owner?"

"He sold us for wieners, but we got away. Then we were caught again."

"I don't understand," says Dumpster Dog. "It wasn't a good restaurant?"

"Don't pay any attention to him," Flat Cat tells them.

The basset hound shrugs. "Just be careful of those treats from the girl with no shoelaces. They'll completely knock you out."

"Someone hit you on the head?" asks Dumpster Dog.

Meanwhile, Flat Cat has been checking things out. "Come on, Dumpster Dog," he says. "Let's go! I'm getting out of here."

"Hold on, Flat Cat! I'm not leaving without my *Parisian Dog* perfume!"

Before Flat Cat can explain how much danger they're in, the three bandits surround them.

The first says, "I'll take the flattened cat; I know someone who collects fried eggs."

The second says, "I'm gonna take the mute parrot; I know a collector who's as deaf as a doorknob."

The third says, "I'm gonna take my time; I don't know which one I want yet."

"I'd like to take care of the dumpy dog," says the little girl with red sneakers.

Immediately, the flies circling Dumpster Dog stop flying and fall onto his snout in shock.

"Sure, squeeze that dog as much as you like, if it'll make you happy. But jeez, kids are really hopeless!" The three bandits roar with laughter.

These owners are so cheerful! thinks Dumpster Dog. *If I ever dig up a bone, I'm going to bring it to them for their museum.*

When Dumpster Dog is finally left alone with the little girl, he's disappointed, because she's sure not squeezing him like a lemon.

"Did I do something wrong?" he asks.

"It's just the opposite, you good doggy. You're going to help me escape."

"But why do you want to leave?"

"Because I was kidnapped by these horrible bandits, and if I don't do exactly what they say, I'll never see my parents again."

"That's a very sad story, little friend, but if I were you, I'd continue to obey my owners."

"Doggy, they will never own me, and I never want to hurt animals again!"

"But how are you going to find your parents? I've already had enough trouble trying to track down my garbage can again."

"Listen, doggy, I know a lot of things, and I know for sure that under your shaggy coat, you are a very remarkable dog."

"If I help you to escape, could you teach me the secret of making puppy-dog eyes?

"No, that's never going to happen."

"Will I still be allowed to have doggy treats?"

"Yes, good doggy, you can have as many treats as you want."

Dumpster Dog weeps for joy, because under his foul-smelling coat there is a brave, kind dog who loves doggy treats.

"I will save everyone!" he tells himself.

Dumpster Dog Falls into a Hole

While the girl turns her poisoned treats into a special cake for the bandits, Dumpster Dog transforms into an escape artist and digs a tunnel for all of his unfortunate friends.

When the clock strikes midnight and the bandits fall off to sleep, dog and cat get ready to go.

"Flat Cat, if everything turns out badly, I want to have told you that you're the flattest cat I've ever known."

"And you, Dumpster Dog, are the dumpiest dog I've ever known."

It's a rough start into the tunnel, as the lame duck slows them down, the alpaca won't stop spitting, and Dumpster Dog keeps mistaking his right for his left and his head for his tail. Nevertheless, he repeats over and over to himself, like a mantra, "I am the can opener of tuna, the shepherd of sheep, a shell for the snail, and I will save my friends!"

Finally, down there in the dank darkness, Dumpster Dog smells something other than sardines, and he senses that the city isn't far away. He scratches hard at the dirt, trying to break through to a glimmer of a streetlamp that will lead them out.

At last, the animals can applaud their hero—all except the penguin, of course.

Then, taking leave, they disperse into the night.

But before heading back to his garbage can with Flat Cat, Dumpster Dog knows that he has one last mission to accomplish.

"What do your parents look like?" he asks the girl.

"My dad is strong and my mom is pretty."

"Do you know where they live?"

"I don't know anymore," says the girl. "All the streets look the same to me, and the city seems so big."

Dumpster Dog thinks for a bit. *Parents can't be found in garbage cans, but they can be found in bakeries at snack time!*

I'm going to take your sneakers," he tells the girl. "You stay here!"

In the morning, Dumpster Dog begins scouring bakeries across the city. He gets hit on the head with jam jars as he goes, but nothing can stop him now! At the fifty-fourth bakery, however, he begins to lose hope. *I'm such a dummy! Her mom surely isn't going to be at a bakery when she doesn't have her little girl anymore. I'm just a spoon*

without yogurt, a hat without a head, a wish-bone with no turkey, and no good for anything!

There's nothing left for Dumpster Dog but to return to his garbage can and pull the lid tight over his head.

But sometimes in the life of a dumpy dog, miracles do happen, and this one comes as the mirage of a woman with shiny shoes, crying on a bench.

Dumpster Dog Lands on His Feet

Poor lady, thinks Dumpster Dog. *If she wasn't wearing shoes, I'd lick her feet to comfort her.*

As he approaches, Dumpster Dog can't keep from asking the woman what's wrong.

"My daughter has been kidnapped, and I'm desperate," she tells him.

"Oh dear, that is so sad," says Dumpster Dog. "I'm sorry, dear lady. Goodbye!"

Dumpster Dog picks up the old sneakers and gets ready to go.

"Wait!" Between sobs, the woman asks, "Where did you find those?"

I didn't know sneakers could make people cry, thinks Dumpster Dog.

In the woman's hand, clenched between her fingers, he sees an old shoelace. At last, he understands!

Dumpster Dog is so moved that he feels like there's a pack of peanuts stuck in his throat, and he can't say a word. He wants to pull the woman by her sleeve, but he's afraid he'll give her rabies, so he just starts running as fast as he can.

When the woman with shiny shoes sees her little girl again, it's Dumpster Dog's turn to weep, this time for joy, right into a garbage can, so as not to disturb them. For the first time in his dumpy life,

Dumpster Dog turns down the reward of a doggy treat. He'd rather have a brand-new bike pump for his friend Flat Cat.

Because in his heart, Dumpster Dog knows that he has found something far better than an owner. From now on, he has a family for life.

www.enchantedlion.com

First English-language edition published in 2019
by Enchanted Lion Books,
67 West Street, 317A, Brooklyn, NY 11222
Originally published in French as *Chien Pourri*
Copyright © 2013 by l'école des loisirs, Paris, France
Copyright © 2019 by Enchanted Lion Books
for the English-language translation & edition
Production and layout: Elynn Cohen
All rights reserved under International and
Pan-American Copyright Conventions
A CIP record is on file with the Library of Congress
ISBN 978-1-59270-252-7 (hardcover)
ISBN 978-1-59270-235-0 (paperback)

1 3 5 7 9 8 6 4 2

Printed in the US by Worzalla, Stevens Point, WI

First Printing

Born in Paris in 1972, Colas Gutman writes his novels in exactly the same position he took as a young boy doing his homework: Stretched out on his bed or perhaps sitting in a chair, using a comic as his desk pad. His first work *Rex, ma Tortue (Rex, My Turtle)* appeared in 2006. Gutman explores childhood and adolescence in his work, with all of the lightness, angst, surrealism, and weirdness that belong to them. In 2013, he invented the hilarious and endearing character of *Chien Pourri (Dumpster Dog)*. The series has been a tremendous success in France since its inception, leading to many volumes and an animated series.

Born in Dijon, France, in 1970, Marc Boutavant is an award-winning illustrator. For years, Boutavant has drawn for picture books and comics, and he's done his fair share of editorial illustration as well. His cartoons and picture books have made him a widely sought after illustrator. Boutavant's lively and expressive illustrations appeal to both children and their parents, for they are playful, probing, and completely endearing all at the same time. His characters for the *Chien Pourri (Dumpster Dog)* series have won the hearts of all French children and are in the process of generating love all over the world. Boutavant lives and works in Paris, France.

Further adventures of

Dumpster Dog,

coming in autumn 2019!

Colas Gutman • Marc Boutavant

Merry Christmas,
Dumpster Dog!

ISBN 978-1-59270-271-8 (hc). $14.95
ISBN 978-1-59270-273-2 (pb). $8.95